To Ajeet, Simer, and Kirpa:
Without your inspiration, thoughts would
have never made it to pen and paper.

To Natasha:
Without your support, this manuscript
would never have blossomed forth into
The Surfing Lesson.

www.bravelionbooks.com

For more information, please contact:
Brave Lion Books
2829 N San Fernando Rd, Unit 101
Los Angeles, CA 90065
bravelionbooks@gmail.com

ISBN: 978-1-7327981-5-1
Library of Congress Control Number: 2021913464

CPSIA Code: PRT0821A

Printed in the United States

THE SURFING LESSON

Written by Bhajneet Singh
Illustrated by Noor Alshalabi

Once upon a time on a beach far away,
lived a family who loved the sea's salt spray.

The kids loved sand between their toes,
and salt water around them—but not up their nose!

In the morning hours, while they were asleep,
their dad with his surfboard would go into the deep.

They'd gaze out the window as he rode the swells,
dreaming of the day they'd be surfers themselves.

One day to the door came three special surprises:
three shiny new surfboards—and just their sizes!

After watching so long, they'd be surfers at last,
but their dad gently smiled and said, "Not so fast!"

"Sit down, my loves, and learn this lesson well:
we must respect the ocean—every wave, every shell."

"Tonight, you'll dream about sun, sand, and sea,
and tomorrow we'll go surfing as a family."

The next morning, they ran to the beach, boards in hand.
But a big WARNING sign had been stuck in the sand.

Trash on the beach and oil on the waves . . .
no time to surf—they had a beach to save!

They took off their wetsuits and began to clean up, but there was too much; they'd have to team up.

So, they held a big rally on the steps of City Hall.
"Our ocean needs help—come one, come all!"

"Hear our lesson and learn it well:
we must respect the ocean—every wave, every shell!"

STOP OCEAN POLLUTION
NO TOXIC WASTE
Evey wave,
every shell!
CREATE SOLUTIONS NOT
POLLUTION
SAVE THE TURTLES

They came in great numbers to lend a hand.
They took oil off the water and trash off the sand.

People of all ages and colors showed great devotion;
even the smallest of us can help save the ocean!

They gathered to pray when the sun had gone down,
and a warm, clean rain washed over the town.

The morning was sunny, the waves were perfect.
Their dad said, "Amazing! Let's go out and surf it!"

They grabbed their boards—dad, mom, sons, and daughter—
and caught their first wave like they were born in the water!

They rode the blue waves again and again.
Their dreams had come true—they were all HANGING TEN!

Their dad's lesson they would remember well:
"We must respect the ocean—every wave, every shell."

A Note to Parents and Kids

Thanks for reading *The Surfing Lesson*. My family and I live in Southern California, and we love going to the beach. The salt water mist, the sound of the waves crashing, the feeling of sand on our feet, and most of all, surfing, bring us a lot of happiness. I would love for children of the future to be able to surf and enjoy the ocean in the same way.

Unfortunately, humans are the biggest threat to our oceans! Every year, we are causing more and more pollution that is damaging what we love. We must be proactive to protect our environment. We can organize beach clean-ups, use recyclable products, and educate others. Each individual can make a huge difference in protecting our oceans, and I hope you will do your part so that we all can surf the waves together for years to come.

With eternal optimism,
Bhajneet Singh